BENITA MY ANGEL

IKECHUKWU OZEME

DEDICATION

This book is dedicated to all single mothers out there and every lover of literary works

CONTENTS

CHAPTER ONE

In a cold snowy morning, emerged a pretty tall and chocolate skinned Lady Craig from the house, in a very thick black sweater that runs down to her thigh and a jean trouser, her hands gloved and her feet in timberland boots. Her head is covered with a thick wool-material cap. Despite her covering her whole body the cold could still slapped her as she emerged from the house prompting her to shrug into herself like a snail hiding in its shell, she turned to rush back into the house but stopped as a thought stroke.

"I can't sit back no matter what", she said inwardly.

She immediately turned and ran hastily out of the compound into the street leaving the gate open. Hastily she dashed into the busy street, running at her possible highest pace without looking back and skipping several odds and huddles by the road. Shortly she got to the heart of the city where cars, taxies and other vehicles formed a strong huddle as one needed to be very careful before taking a step across the road or be forced to kiss the soil by a knock from the vehicles.

Lady Craig carelessly ran across the road and almost got knocked down by a taxi which pulled up quickly and luckily avoided the fatality. While the driver was busy cursing and calling her names, she never turned back and kept running like an animal being chased by a hunter.

Everyone who saw her would believe she was running to get hold of her life and yes, she certainly was. She just got a text from the Proprietor of the boarding school where her daughter schools that due to a perceived natural disaster, the school has decided to vacate all the pupils, hence every parent and guardian is expected to come take their children home. Lady Craig's heart skipped at reading the text and she knew her whole life lies in the hands of her daughter; she cherished her daughter so much that she would never spend a whole day without visiting to know how she was faring in school.

Lady Craig's daughter, Benita was her one and only child and the only companion she had for that reason, she preferred receiving a bullet to a pin pinching any part of her daughter's body.

"She is my life madam, if anything happens to her, consider me a dead body. She is the air that I breath every second, please take good care of her for me", Lady Craig warned the school Proprietor the day she registered Benita in school.

Within a short time, Lady Craig arrived Benita's school and ran straight to the classroom and it was empty, she hastily ran back to the hostel and everywhere was locked up already, to worsen issues, there was neither a pupil at sight nor the voice of anyone heard within the compound. The world seemed to have ended for Lady Craig who turned and ran down the corridor of the hostel and dashed across the school compound into the Proprietor's office to behold her daughter, Benita who happily jumped up and embraced her.

"Good morning Lady Craig", the Proprietor greeted.

"Good morning dear lady, thanks for securing her for me", she replied.

"It is my duty; however, I am so sorry for stressing you this cold morning".

"Anything done by me for the sake of my daughter is rather joyous and not stress, thanks for the text".

"You are welcome madam. Please bear with us, a natural disaster has been perceived and it will be safe to vacate all the pupils. Meanwhile you have got no reason to be pissed, arrangement has been made for the final classes to finish their remaining papers online through the school portal and your daughter is one of them, in essence, the vacation won't have any effect on her or any other pupil as all academic activities would still continue".

"Wow, a nice move by the school authority".

Lady Craig and the Proprietor spent a few minutes chatting in the office. Later on, the Proprietor drove them home.

CHAPTER TWO

Lady Craig is a young single mother of thirty nine years. She got married to her late husband when she was twenty six and in a few months, she was already pregnant. Her joy knew no bound as her dream of carrying her husband's baby was nearing fulfillment. She loved and cherished the unborn baby and always prayed that it would be a baby girl at birth.

Mr Craig her late husband was her lover from their college days, they were classmates from college but later went separate ways as she went for teaching school while Mr Craig went ahead to study Electrical Engineering in one of the Universities in the city. Though they were no longer within physical reach, they never spent a day without talking to each other. Mr Craig would wake up every morning to the smile of receiving heart-warming love texts from her and he would try to reciprocate the following morning. That way, their love for each other grew stronger every day.

Mr Craig was first to graduate and on his fiancé's graduation day, he travelled down to her school and proposed to her before the whole world, that marked the beginning of the fulfillment of her dream of carrying his baby one day.

Months went by and it was time to be delivered of the baby. Mr Craig was busy at work when he got a call from his wife that she needed his attention and on his way hurrying home, he got knocked down by a car and was rushed to the hospital immediately. Lady Craig waited and waited for him to return but didn't see him, called his line severally but he didn't pick, she had to help herself, she managed to go down to a nearby hospital where she was successfully delivered of baby Benita. She was so happy and excited but her joy didn't last long as the news of the passing out of her husband was broken to her on her return from the hospital.

After mourning her husband, it didn't take long for her to transfer the love she had for her husband to her daughter and little Benita never failed in putting a smile on Lady Craig's face, everyday.

CHAPTER THREE

Though she was a teacher in one of the government-

owned schools in their locality, life was not totally easy for

Lady Craig financially as her monthly salary was not enough

for her to take care of herself and her daughter including

paying rents and spending on other necessary and unforeseen

circumstances. She however never allowed Benita to lack anything; she would pretend to be very okay while dying inside to ensure that her daughter is properly taken care of.

As soon as Benita was five years, she enrolled her in one of the best schools within and as soon as she was done with junior primary school, Lady Craig was very pleased with her academic performance and took yet a difficult decision which was getting her enrolled in the very best school in the entire Local Government Area.

"Benita my Angel" Lady Craig started; I am so pleased by your ability to be the second best pupil in your class despite all odds".

"Thank you so much mummy, it's my pleasure to make you happy".

"And I can't wait to see you fly higher; I have decided to enroll you in McCarthy Group of Schools where you can obtain more standard education"

A very happy Benita jumped up in jubilation as if she had always wanted to study in McCarthy.

"Thank you so much mummy, I really can't express how happy I feel now with words", Benita appreciated.

"For making your mother happy, you deserve to be made happy too, as soon as the next term starts, you will be moving to McCarthy".

"Dear mummy, you have always called me your angel and this time, I want to promise to be that angel to you, for putting this smile on my face, mummy, I promise to put a smile on your face through my academic performances.

Lady Craig was marveled at her daughter's words, she quickly embraced her and tears of joy shortly ran down her cheek.

Things are however easier said than done, it was never difficult for Lady Craig to make the decision and promise but the resources to back it was the challenge. Being aware of her low income, Lady Craig decided to quit the teaching work and start up a business with the little money she had saved from her salary. It was a right one for her as she would make profit worth almost her monthly salary in three weeks or less.

Quitting her white-collar job was one of the greatest sacrifices she ever made to achieve an aim because from childhood, Lady Craig loved teaching so much and already took a decision to be a teacher for the rest of her life but since it had to do with ensuring her daughter's happiness by giving her the best, she had to put her love for teaching aside and face reality.

It was soon time for a new term to start and Lady Craig was gradually preparing for the enrollment of her daughter in McCarthy which was the best school in the entire Local Government. Unlike other schools in the area, McCarthy was a Private Mission School with quality teachers and learning environment, good recreational facilities and standard educational facilities too. The school was severally commended by the state government for the high quality of education it provided for the pupils. The consisted of day and boarding and Benita was enrolled for boarding to enable her read and concentrate on her studies very well. She was however branded the petty boarder because unlike other

boarding pupils, she sees her mother

every day.

CHAPTER FOUR

It was Benita's final year as a pupil in the school and they were already in the exam period when a natural disaster was perceived to take place within the school area and to be on a safe side, the school authority decided that the pupils and teachers including other staff would vacate the school and converted the manual learning process to E-learning.

Lady Craig returned home with Benita and began tutoring her on the use of computer while she prepared for the E-learning and forth coming examination. Early in the morning, Lady Craig would ensure that Benita was well fed, provide her meal for the day before going out for her daily business, she would return daily and meet Benita seriously busy with her studies.

"Benita my angel", she called on her return one day, "do you take out time to rest from reading at all?"

"Yes mummy, I do but a little time though", she replied.

"Please, easy on yourself so you don't over stress your brain".

"I am fine mummy, I am simply moved by the zeal to come out in flying colors at the end of the examination and ensure I fulfilled the promise I made to you that I will make you happy".

"That's my angel, I can't be less proud of you".

Benita never gave herself much resting time as she was busy preparing for the examination that would commence soon. And soon, it was time for the examination, Lady Craig would spend more time at home to guide her through but Benita never allowed her close once the examination starts. She handled the computer herself and would shut it down after each day's E-examination.

When results were out, the state government was marveled by Benita's outstanding performance as she outscored everyone in the state, hence she was offered a scholarship to continue her studies in a better country and her mother too received a huge support from the government which enabled her to travel out of the country with her daughter.

ABOUT THE AUTHOR

IKECHUKWU OZEME

Ikecchukwu Ozeme is a Graduate of Theatre And Film Studies, University of Nigeria, Nsukka. He is a renowned writer with several novels, poems and drama texts to his credit. He is also a Nollywood screenwriter with over twenty movies to his credit. His love and passion for writing is highly

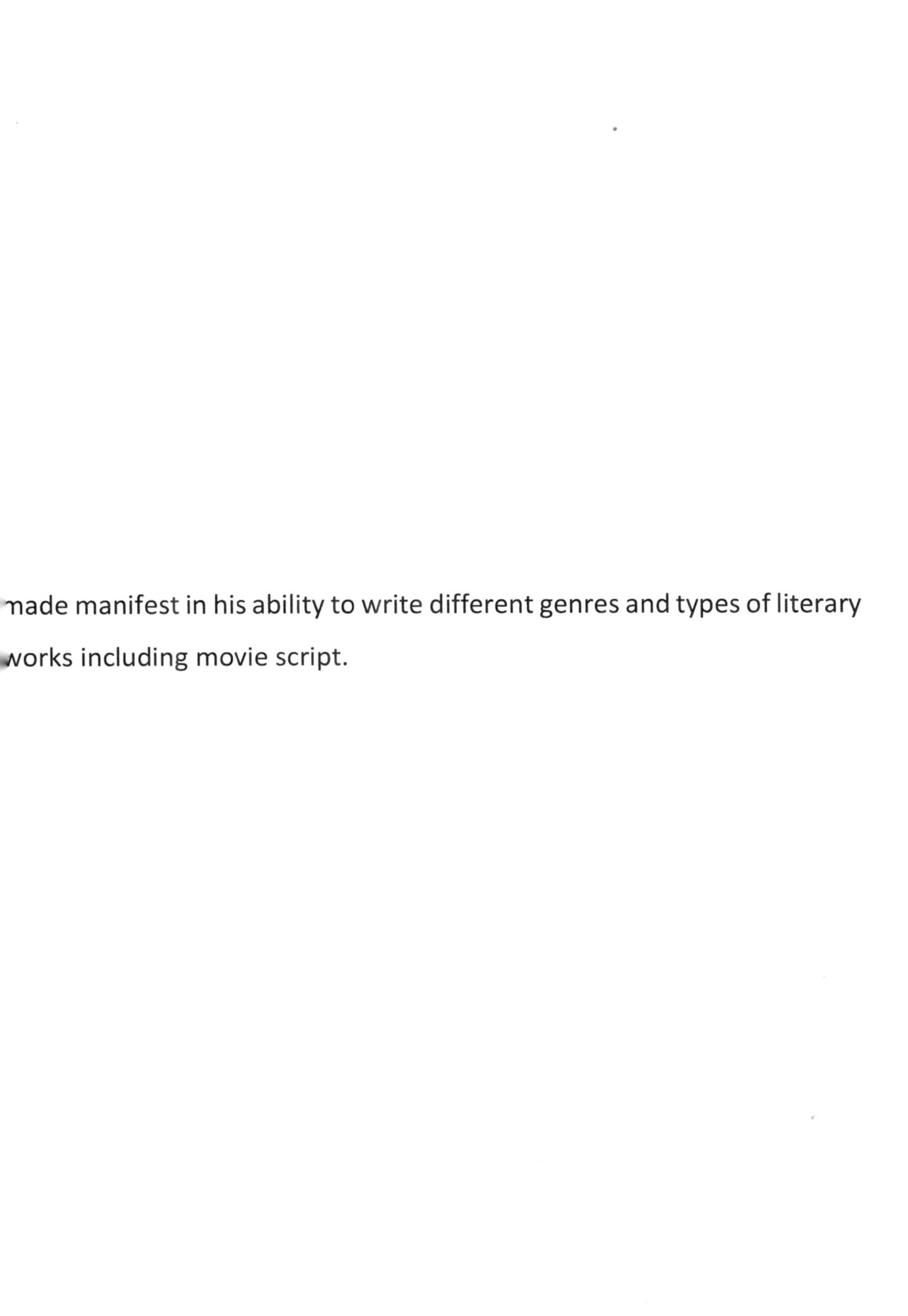

made manifest in his ability to write different genres and types of literary works including movie script.

www.ingramcontent.com/pod-product-compliance
Lightning Source LLC
Chambersburg PA
CBHW071257140726
47996CB00007B/2886